For Gea,
who has contributed much to the creation of this book.
— C.C.

Original title: Otto Karotto
Originally published in Austria by:
Picus Verlag Ges.m.b.H., Vienna
© 2000 Picus Verlag Ges.m.b.H., Vienna

This edition published in 2011 in the United States of America
by Eerdmans Books for Young Readers,
an imprint of
Wm. B. Eerdmans Publishing Co.
2140 Oak Industrial Dr. NE, Grand Rapids, Michigan 49505
P.O. Box 163, Cambridge CB3 9PU U.K.

www.eerdmans.com/youngreaders

Manufactured at Tien Wah Press in Singapore, February 2011, first edition

17 16 15 14 13 12 11   8 7 6 5 4 3 2 1

Library of Congress Cataloging-in-Publication Data

Carrer, Chiara.
[Otto Karotto. English]
Otto Carrotto / written and illustrated by Chiara Carrer.
p. cm.
Summary: Otto the rabbit decides to eat nothing but carrots,
causing unexpected consequences.
ISBN 978-0-8028-5393-6 (alk. paper)
[1. Rabbits — Fiction. 2. Carrots — Fiction.] I. Title.
PZ7.C43224Ot 2011
[E] — dc22
2010049546

Otto CARRotto

Chiara Carrer

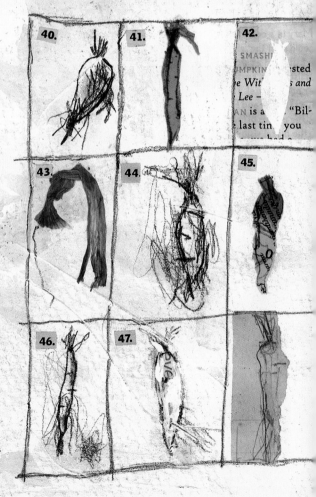

Eerdmans Books for Young Readers
Grand Rapids, Michigan • Cambridge, U.K.

Rabbits are strange! Otto thinks.
They all have their own quirks.
For example, there's Trixie, Otto's sister.
She will only wear **red shoes**.
Red shoes every day.
No shoes but **red shoes**!

And then there's Willie, Otto's best friend.
Ever since he got his **blue roller skates**,
he will not take them off!
He never has anything else on his mind,
or on his feet.
He even wears his
blue roller skates
to bed at night!

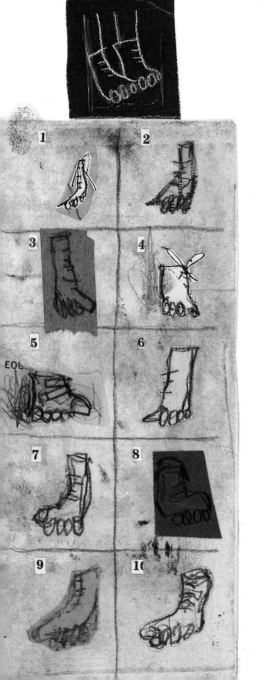

But Otto is a rabbit too.
So he thinks it over.
And one morning
at breakfast
he says, "**Carrots**!
From now on
I will only eat
carrots.

Carrots and nothing else!"

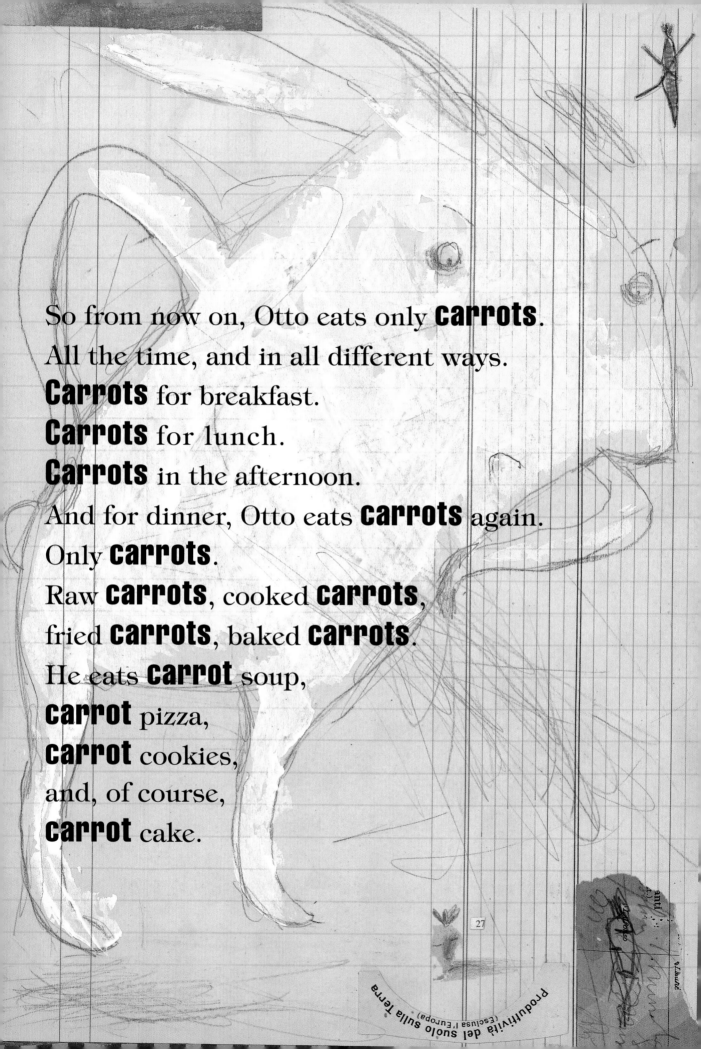

So from now on, Otto eats only **carrots**.
All the time, and in all different ways.
Carrots for breakfast.
Carrots for lunch.
Carrots in the afternoon.
And for dinner, Otto eats **carrots** again.
Only **carrots**.
Raw **carrots**, cooked **carrots**,
fried **carrots**, baked **carrots**.
He eats **carrot** soup,
carrot pizza,
carrot cookies,
and, of course,
carrot cake.

Otto does not want
to eat anything
else. It is no use
when his mother and father,
his grandmas and grandpas,
and his aunts and uncles
try to talk to him.

You'll turn into a carrot!

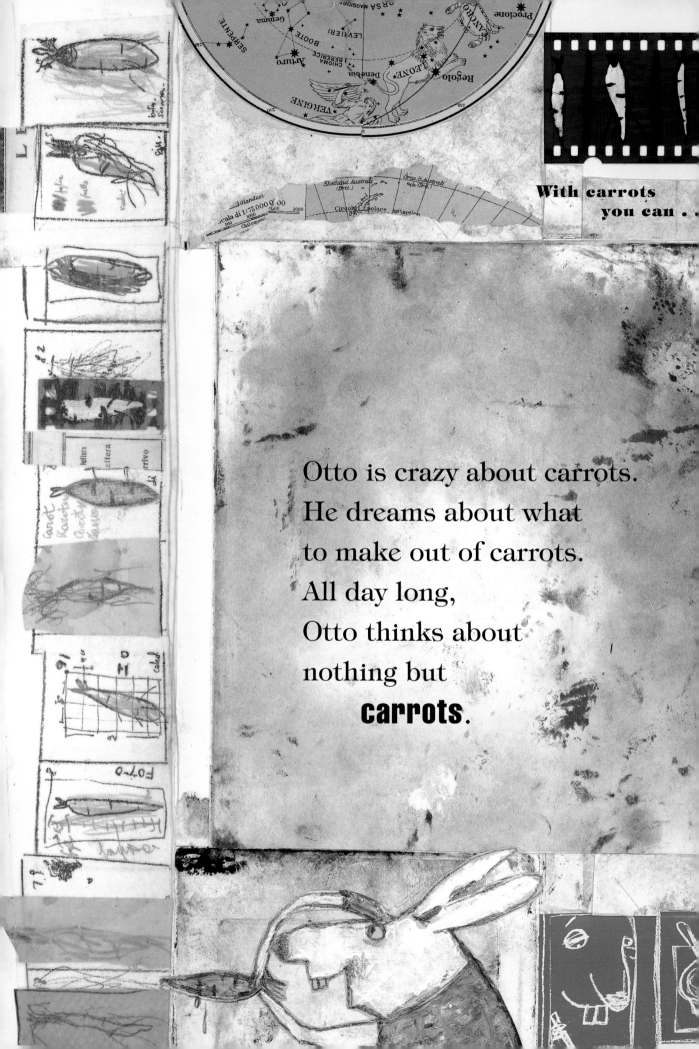

With carrots
you can . .

Otto is crazy about carrots.
He dreams about what
to make out of carrots.
All day long,
Otto thinks about
nothing but
carrots.

peek through walls, find a needle in a haystack, see into my heart.

What you can do with carrots . . . .

A carrot boat

A carrot airplane

A carrot car

A carrot rocket

A carrot house

And because Otto is thinking about nothing but **carrots**, he doesn't realize that he has changed.

"Oh, no!"

Willie and Trixie are
suddenly crazy about
Otto's ears.
Trixie is nibbling on them.
Every rabbit likes
carrots
now and then,
but this is going too far!
Then it gets worse . . .

On the first day of school,
Otto's classmates dance around him
and tease him:
"Otto Carrotto! Otto Carrotto!"
They laugh at him and stare at his ears
as if they would like to take a bite
out of them.

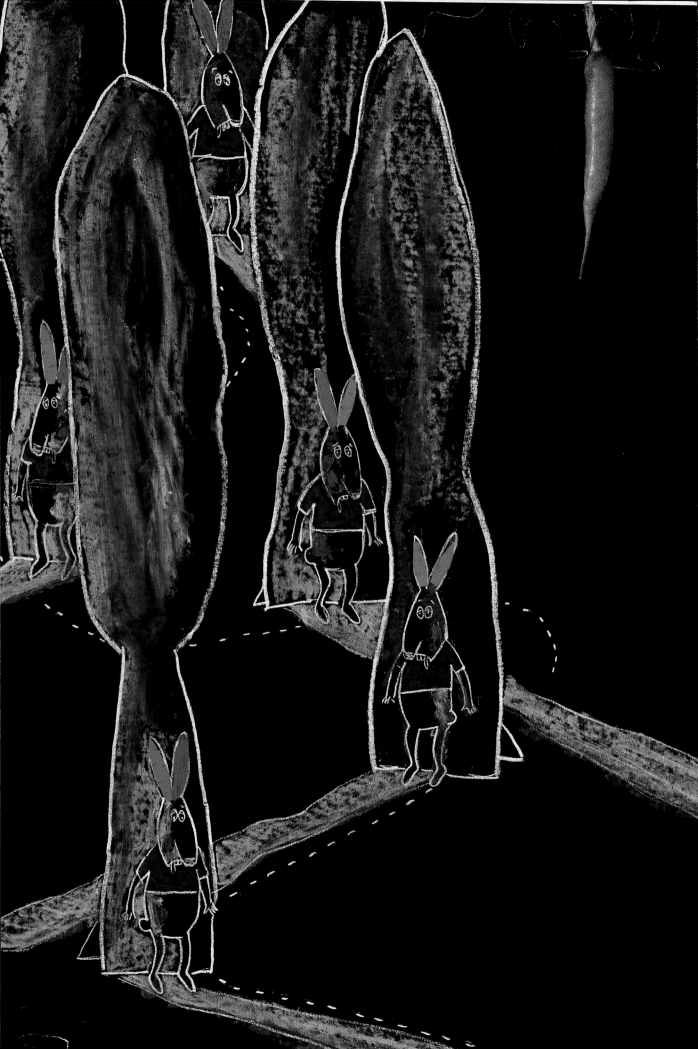

Otto runs away.
He is afraid and
hides behind the trees.
What will happen now?
He doesn't dare
go back to school.
Does everybody think
he is a **carrot**?
And does everybody
want to nibble
on him?
He can't hide
from the
other rabbits
forever!

He looks around, surprised.
Even the trees look like huge
carrot monsters.
Oh dear, have his eyes
gone bad from
all the **carrots**?
There is only one thing
that will help.
No more carrots!
Otto does not want
to eat a single carrot
ever again.

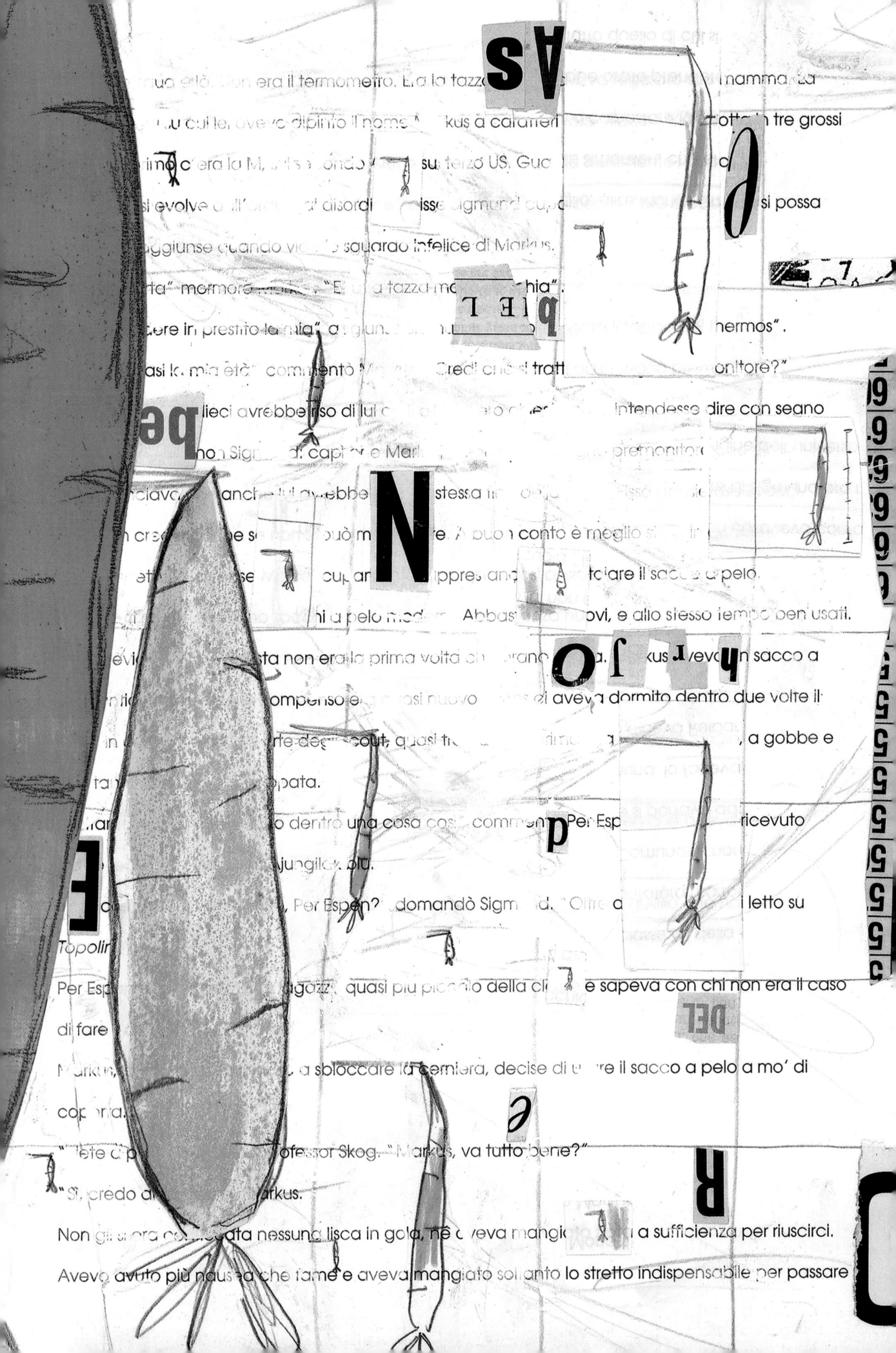

...ra il termometro. Era la tazza... ...mamma la

...u cui le avevo dipinto il nome ...kus a caratteri... ...otta in tre grossi

...imo c'era la M, il secondo A... su... terzo US. Gua... ...si possa

...si evolve dall'ora... ai disordini... isse Sigmund cup... ...

...aggiunse quando vide lo squarcio infelice di Markus.

...ta" mormorò Mark... "È una tazza mol... ...chia".

...ere in prestito la mia" a... ...hermos".

...asi k. mia età" commentò M... "Credi che si tratt... ...onitore?"

...lieci avrebbe riso di lui c... ...o che... ...ntendesse dire con seano

...non Sig... d. capir... e Mark... ...premonitore

...iava... anch... lui avrebbe... stessa... ...Fissò...

...n cre... be s... può... re. A buon conto è meglio... in...

...et... sse... cup... ...ippres... ...ciare il sacco a pelo.

...hi a pelo mod... Abbast... ...ovi, e allo stesso tempo ben usati.

...evi... sta non era la prima volta ch... erano... ...kus aveva un sacco a

...nti... ompenso e quasi nuovo... ...ei aveva dormito dentro due volte il

...in... ...rte degli scout, quasi tr... rim... ...a gobbe e

...ta... opata.

...ar... o dentro una cosa così" commen... Per Esp... ricevuto

...jungila... più.

...c... Per Espen? domandò Sigm... d. "Oltre a... ...letto su

Topolir...

Per Esp... ...agazz... quasi più piccolo della cl... e sapeva con chi non era il caso

di fare...

Mark... ...a sbloccare la cerniera, decise di u... re il sacco a pelo a mo' di

cop... ...ria.

"...ete c p... ...ofessor Skog. "Markus, va tutto bene?"

"Sì, credo... ...arkus.

Non gli ancora c... ...ata nessuna lisca in gola, né aveva mangia... ...a sufficienza per riuscirci.

Avevo avuto più nausea che fame e avevo mangiato soltanto lo stretto indispensabile per passare

Otto puts his cap over his **carrot** ears
and runs to the supermarket.
He fills the shopping cart
up to the brim with . . .
spinach!
Now Otto eats only **spinach**.
All the time, and in all different ways.
Strained **spinach**, baked **spinach**,
fried **spinach**, and **spinach** pie.

.9

Hurray for **spinach**!

Spinach

is the

best!

E Car
Carrer, Chiara
Otto Carrotto /